Tipping Point
Ecofiction for Tomorrow's World

Edited by

M.A. Dosser

Cover & Interior Artwork by

Kevin Pabst

THE CURB CENTER

Editing by M.A. Dosser

ISBN : 979-8-9928061-0-6

Table of Contents:

Foreword
By Em Palughi

There is no shortage of writing about grief. If you have
lost someone, you may have been surprised at the flood tide
of writing that was suddenly at your door: obituaries, funeral
speeches, eulogies, uncomfortable text messages to old
friends, memorial Facebook posts, remains release forms,
post-it notes stuck to your bathroom mirror that say *you are a
person* and *you will be okay* and *brush your hair,* etc. Death is one
of the epic subjects of human history, an abstraction so
tangible our instinct is to personify it: "Because I could not
stop for Death — / He kindly stopped for me —" says Emily
Dickinson.

What, then, can writers do when death is ongoing at an
unimaginable scale? When it goes beyond the individual and
encompasses entire species, ecosystems, and land masses?
Despite being part of the cultural consciousness for decades,
it seems climate disaster is resisting this kind of literary
obsession. Poet and bioregionalist Gary Snyder put it this way
in *Practice of The Wild:*

The extinction of a species, each one a pilgrim of four billion years of evolution, is an irreversible loss. The ending of the lines of so many creatures with whom we have traveled this far is an occasion of profound sorrow and grief. Death can be accepted and to some degree transformed. But the loss of lineages and all their future young is not something to accept. It must be rigorously and intelligently resisted.

Snyder points out the key difference between individual and ecological grief: the stage of acceptance. A healthy cycle of grief ends here: the final act of five, an acceptance that something has been lost that was always going to be lost. Climate change, however, was never inevitable—these are losses that can and must be stopped. And so climate change is less easily transformed and processed in our writing, more difficult to press into the shape of a metaphor or a narrative. It is this ongoing and tragic complexity that makes ecopoetry and ecofiction so difficult.

Some might mistake climate apathy for a kind of acceptance. This is a grave error: this "acceptance" that there is nothing to be done about climate disaster at all, that end-of-the-world doomerist rhetoric, might lull the entire population into inaction if not properly combatted. It is not a result of great feeling, as the acceptance stage of grief is, but a result of a capacity to feel that has been totally exhausted. While detrimental to the cause, it is understandable why so many have succumbed to this way of thinking: death at such an enormous scale requires enormous grieving. As Liza Featherstone says in "How to Live in a Burning World Without Losing Your Mind,"

> The way out of this confusion is neither feel-good solutionism nor submitting to the apocalypse. Instead, we need to learn to make space, in our conversations, activism, and media, for feeling grief, anxiety, guilt, and fear about climate change, no matter how difficult or dark.

That is why climate literature is so important: it creates space for processing eco-grief. It is an effective balm for the wound of climate apathy. Writing is a powerful tool for us mourners: the elegy allows us to make a collective of ourselves, to come together in loss and recover. In Elizabeth Bishop's poem "One Art," she is so convinced that writing is integral to mourning that she slips in a command midline, in parentheses: "the art of losing's not too hard to master / though it may look like (*Write* it!) like disaster." This acknowledgement of loss can lead to the healing that makes us better activists: if we keep moving through this loss without taking a moment for mourning, we will burn out long before the work is done.

Grief is associated with the past and memory, understandably. Death writing is often concerned with remembering, preserving, and imagining a past with a dead person. A central part of getting through grief, however, is imagining a future. *What do you want your relationship with his memory to be?* asked my therapist after the death of my father.

How does he fit into the rest of your life? For someone in mourning, part of the task is to imagine a life post-death. For eco-writers, imagining a future at all is radical. This makes speculative fiction a particularly effective tool: the inclusion of the impossible makes the possible even clearer.

Rachel Carson knew to capture the imagination of the public, she had to invoke their ability to predict the future. Her scientific evidence against the harmful pesticide DDT was impressive, but what catapulted her book to public awareness was her imagined future: a "Silent Spring," as her pivotal book is titled. This imagined future created direct action: the brown pelican, once on the brink of extinction, is now as common a sight on the Gulf Coast as a seagull or a tourist.

The works in this anthology are doing the same thing: they imagine worlds where there is no sun, where the sun bakes people inside their homes, where oxygen is only available at a premium. Still, the characters that inhabit this anthology survive and fight for the living things around them. This anthology holds space for mourning during a time when the emotional toll of climate change is often dismissed. Each story, in this way, is a radical act of care for both the planet and for readers.

Slice of Life

By Thomas J. Griffin

About the author:
Thomas J. Griffin is a life-long fiction lover and sumo wrestling enthusiast who lives in Nashville, Tennessee and writes out of an attic that could use more natural light. He is the editor of *Flash Point SF* and his own stories have appeared in publications such as *Daily Science Fiction*, *100-Foot Crow*, and *Wyldblood Press*.

Slice of Life
By Thomas J. Griffin

Routine was important. Though it had been years since he'd seen a sunrise (or the sun at all for that matter), Earl's alarm clock still went off every morning at 6:00am, and he never hit snooze more than twice.

This time he was up with the first buzz.

The smell of fresh, auto-brewed coffee helped draw Earl across the room, his only pitstop at the stainless-steel urinal between his bed and the kitchenette. He depressed the flush, listened to the vacuum *whoosh* of liquid waste rushing away through the pipes toward the water reclaimer. Then it was off to the cupboard for a clean mug.

If God had still been listening, Earl would have thanked him for coffee. Instead he thanked himself for stockpiling as much as he could pack into the larder. While letting the caffeine do its work, he thumbed through an old copy of *Rolling Stone*, occasionally stopping to read a feature or study a picture. There was nothing within the magazine's covers he hadn't seen a dozen times over, but it was better than staring at the wall, and he liked to challenge himself to notice something new each time, even the smallest detail. A typo. Anything.

It was getting more and more difficult.

When at last he felt fully awake, Earl got up from his seat, setting the *Rolling Stone* aside as a coaster for the cooling dregs of his coffee, and had himself a good, invigorating stretch. Then he made his way over to the clothes rack, stepped into the hazmat suit, and turned toward the blast door.

One by one the tumblers clicked until the door fell open quietly on well-oiled hinges. The tunnel lights were motion-sensitive—they popped on as he approached, then winked out thirty seconds after he'd passed, give or take. Energy conservation was the name of the game, though today Earl was in no hurry.

It was a two-minute walk uphill to the outer blast door. Like the one behind, this door was as thick as an armoire, lead-lined, and could only be unlocked from the inside—a clever but useless feature, as no one had ever tried to get in. Unlike its predecessor, this door had a window, and because of that Earl made the trek up to the surface every morning. What he saw outside never changed, but he had to check anyway.

Earl slid back the protective steel panel and gazed out through quadruple-paned glass. He'd built his fallout bunker on unincorporated land outside what had once been Cottontown, Tennessee, a rural oasis halfway between Nashville and Bowling Green, Kentucky, and he could still remember what it used to look like. Today was May 6th (the calendar claimed). In a normal year, everything would have been in full bloom, entire fields springing up fresh and green overnight after a spring storm. The pollen count would be through the roof, antihistamines a must. His old three-bedroom ranch had sat a half-mile off the road, nestled between pasture and wood and just far enough away from civilization that clear nights were near as bright as the day, the Moon crowded by so many stars the eye lost focus trying to keep track. It had been a quiet life, slow but peaceful. Earl's nearest neighbors had been miles down the road, if you didn't count the local robin who built her nest atop the jamb above Earl's front door every March. About this time she would be pushing her chicks out of said nest, scattering faded blue bits of eggshell all over the porch.

Nothing from that memory remained. Instead, a tundra of mottled grays, muted by an eternal twilight, freezing winds scattering fat white snowflakes and specks of ash over the barren hills.

The familiar madness crept over Earl at the sight. His hand strayed toward the locking mechanism, coming to rest upon it gradually, delicately. He could look no more; today would be the day he turned the latch and stepped outside. The radiation had dissipated, but the cold had not. Even with the suit on, he wouldn't last more than a few minutes, and after years breathing the same recycled air, that was no time at all. He'd built this bunker to survive, but it had done its job too well; Earl had outlasted the world, and now, every day, he asked himself what for.

For the hope of warmer days, came a thought in answer. This voice, too, was familiar. It sounded like his wife, Monica. Though he'd not seen her in so long, it was always her voice in his head talking him off the ledge.

Was she still out there somewhere? Was she still holding out hope for him?

A speck of green caught Earl's eye. He blinked, sure his desperate mind had imagined it amidst all that gray, but no. A clover shoot, pushing up through the ashen soil.

Earl lifted his hand off the mechanism, slid the window panel closed again, then regressed down the tunnel.

With the inner blast door closed firmly behind him, Earl stepped out of the hazmat suit and hung it back on the rack. Then he went over to the cupboard to inspect his stores. Routine was important. At 6:45am every morning, Earl ate breakfast.

At 7:00am he turned on the two-way radio and began checking stations.

Another Sunshine Day

By Monic Ductan

About the author:

Monic Ductan is the author of *Daughters of Muscadine*, a story collection that won the Weatherford Award and the Tennessee Book Award. She teaches at Tennessee Tech University.

Another Sunshine Day
By Monic Ductan

A body cooling suit. The most deluxe model. Only $399. Everyone needs one, a craze that started around the year 2060 when winter stopped coming. Our temperatures have rarely fallen below fifty degrees since that year. We haven't seen snow in a decade here in Nashville. Luckily, my husband Devon and I each have a cooling suit, but now those suits don't feel like enough. Some days it feels like the earth itself will crack open and melt.

Devon and I have been Zooming together every day since he got stuck in Philly. Two weeks ago, he drove up there to visit his mama, and another heat wave hit unexpectedly. Temperatures in the 120s, and he couldn't get safe transportation home. He doesn't have one of those newer cars that block UV rays.

I open the Zoom app on my phone and sign on to the scheduled meeting. Devon and I are both punctual, we usually sign on around the same time. Today, he's late. I wait a few minutes and then text him a reminder. When he doesn't answer back right away, I start to worry.

I call his phone. Straight to voicemail.

We are in November already, but in the past couple of weeks I've seen the news stories about folks having fainting spells as they walk to their mailboxes or try to visit neighbors. Going out in these temperatures can be deadly without a cooling suit, and even though Devon has one, I still don't want him to risk it.

Where is he?

Just as I'm about to call him again, Devon's camera comes on the Zoom and I instantly start to blow him kisses. He laughs and catches them. Devon is a handsome man with large cheek apples and a bright shine to his brown eyes. I've always admired his hair. Sure, the black hair on his head is fine, but I also admire that his eyebrows are naturally arched, and he keeps his beard neatly trimmed. He hasn't been to a barber in weeks, but I can see he's maintained the beard and hair at his mama's place.

"I can't wait to see you," he says. "I wish I could come tomorrow."

"You better wait until next week," I tell him. "It's supposed to get down to about a hundred degrees then."

"I know," he says, the frustration leaking out of his voice. "But what if it doesn't?"

Back in '55, I started stocking up this basement of ours with food enough to last a few months. This way, I don't have to go out to the grocery at all during summertime, the most brutal season. Last year, we had a few days where the temp got up high enough to make your eyes and skin burn.

"How are you holding up?" he asks me.

"I'm hanging in here." I sigh and say, "I can't tell you how glad I am that we both work from home."

People who do service jobs have a much more difficult time. Having to leave the house in their special-made cars and body suits is undoubtedly stressful, and that is compounded when they are mandated to take furlough time on the hottest days.

He nods. "I've stopped following the Texas story. It's unreal," he says.

Out in Texas, the power grid failed and people roasted inside their houses. Cable news channels and social media are all filled with their stories. Thousands dead. Bodies parched in living rooms and laying sprawled atop freezers.

I stretch out on my back on the sofa. We stare at each other through our screens, and I can almost feel the longing emanating from Devon's body. We've been married twenty-four years and have never been apart for more than two weeks at a time. "Don't worry so much," he tells me, reading my mind like he often does.

We blow kisses back and forth until we hang up the phone.

People aren't sleeping soundly enough. They say the heat impacts our ability to dream. I hardly ever remembered my dreams before the world got so hot. Now, I occasionally remember one. The dream starts with a visit from our daughter, Marnie. She drives up from Atlanta, and Devon and I take her to an ice cream parlor. We sit outside the parlor under a shade tree and lick our cones. Half chocolate and half coffee bean for me. Cookies and cream for Marnie. Strawberry for Devon. There's no burning sun. It's dusk and cool. In the dream, we luxuriate in our ability to sit outdoors. In reality, I haven't seen Marnie in person in almost two years. She's one of those young people who refuses to go outside, and Devon and I are so caught up in worrying over the weather that we haven't made the trek down to Georgia in what feels like forever.

I have that dream again and again. Sometimes I fantasize about it while I'm awake. Sitting outside with people I love. Enjoying the weather and the ice cream. Laughing.

Just as predicted, the temp falls down to ninety-nine on Wednesday of the following week. Devon texts when he's on the way, and I start getting ready. I paint my nails, shampoo my hair. I haven't cooked in weeks because it makes the house so darned hot. Today, I make pasta and grilled chicken. I roast some Brussels sprouts and drizzle them with honey.

Knowing that Devon will be here at any moment, I go out to the screen porch to wait.

There is an old church song called "Another Sunshine Day." I grew up in a Black Baptist church, but I'm not religious as an adult. Still, those old songs always come out of me when I'm feeling joy. I don't know the lyrics of this one, only the refrain of "A-noth-er Sun-shine Da-ay!!" I keep humming those words to myself until I see his black SUV climbing the hill at the bottom of our long driveway. "A-noth-er Sun-shine-y Da-ay!!" I scream as I go down the steps to meet him.

The world is burning, but I remember another spiritual:

I'm. So. GLAD!

Trouble don't last AL-WA-AYS...

I close my eyes and lean into his embrace.

Hatfield and Son's Affordable Aquatic Abodes

By David Cole

About the author:

David Cole (or ColedOne) is a writer and multimedia artist from Appalachia who spent his formative years growing up on both sides of the Kentucky-Tennessee border. His work spans video essays, fiction, and poetry in both the literary and gaming spaces. He is very proud of his YouTube work, which seeks to highlight the narrative strengths and oddities of video games.

Hatfield and Son's Affordable Aquatic Abodes
By David Cole

"Old world won't do you any good, son."

The words were punctuated by a wet plop as the refurbished music player, and the mercifully cushioned headphones attached to it, broke the surface of the New Atlantic. They sank, immediately, and the faint muffle of the shoegaze track Tanner had been enjoying was drowned out by the murky water and churning engine. He looked to his father with an unbelieving anger. Don confidently stood at the wheel as if he had not just steered too close to yet another bank. The only thing that had kept Tanner from pushing the old man over the railing of their home atop the waves had been the music he'd been hoarding. And now? It was short-circuiting underwater, or perhaps offering a passing fish insight into the garage scene of the mid-aughts.

"We're going where the real music is made! Nashville is the epicenter of the industry!" Don shouted over the ambient noise of the ship.

Tanner responded through grit teeth, "That's only because

LA went under."

Don ignored his son's remark and continued the sales pitch, "Think about it! The coastline is about to meet the biggest—" Tanner interjected quietly here with the word "remaining," but Don cleared his throat and continued, "Biggest *remaining* music scene in these twenty-seven United States. Opportunity like this does not knock often. And that's why Hatfield and Son's Affordable Aquatic Abodes will cruise right into the Cumberland Harbor and change the real estate landscape of America's largest cultural hub."

Tanner gripped the railing lining the side of the *Kevin Costner* until his knuckles went white. His eyes remained locked on the spot where his music had been lost to him, rapidly diminishing in the rippled trail of the ship and its towline. Dragged behind were about twenty other sloops of varying size and effectiveness. Each had been retrofitted, painstakingly, by himself, his father, and his grandfather before them. They'd been turned into houseboats, now available for sale to the less wealthy denizens of the cities they passed on repeat voyages up and down the coast. Each town typically saw their empty entourage shrink by a vessel or two, until his father inevitably spotted someone's old fishing junker and saw what he called "the spirit within." That always led to several days of labor for Tanner, having to clean out whatever detritus had built up over God only knew how long.

"Stop moping, Tanner! Once we've rolled into Nashville, I'll find you a new player. One with a better selection. Waylon, Willie… All the Hank Williamses, Senior through the Sixth."

Don stood particularly straight, his hands wrapped around the *Kevin Costner's* wheel. He knew that these were the promises that guaranteed a father his son's respect.

Tanner, turning to his father with fire in his eyes, asked the prescient question: "With what money?"

"Don't be stupid, son, we're going to be drowning in it once those yokels get a look at what we're hauling."

Somewhere behind them, a mast rising from one of the refitted trawlers clipped an overhanging branch from the tree line and cracked tremendously. Don cursed aloud as he wheeled around to take stock of the damage, shrugged, and continued to pilot the ship along.

"Speaking of our fortunes, have you revised the financing plans like I asked?" Don questioned his son with a tone that they both had come to recognize as a prelude to disappointment.

"I had a question about them, actually," Tanner replied.

Don widened his eyes in surprise, having expected a flat "no." He looked over to the boy, still drooped over the railing and excitedly spoke, "Lay it on me."

Tanner turned his back on his father, pacing toward a table bolted against the cabin and the documents he'd weighed down with various rocks of differing origins. Pushing aside a particularly lovely one he'd picked up on the shores of the Erie, where Pittsburgh once had been, he searched the paper for the line he'd been having trouble with.

"With the interest rate you're proposing, very few people we do business with would ever be able to actually *own* the boats. I figure it must have been a mistake. It's down as twenty-five but surely you meant two-point-five?"

Don laughed and continued to ignore the dragging noise that had been dogging them since that collision with the tree. "No, no, that's correct. It's kind of a subscription model I'd like to try. We sell the boat to them for a lowered opening payment, then collect interest as long as they live aboard. When they pass it off to some other worker, or their children —whatever—the interest will diminish, but carry on. So we continue to earn well into your time at the helm. I call it 'generating generational revenue.'" Don swept out a hand as he used his own terminology, adding the slightest hint of razzle-dazzle to the description.

Tanner stood in silence as the *Kevin Costner* continued to cruise along the coastline, utterly unaffected by either razzle or dazzle. "Dad…" He began, but was unsure of how to finish. The words were caught in his throat. "No one can take that deal."

"They won't have a choice, son. There are very few places to live these days, fewer every year. Enterprising salesmen like ourselves are only going to be able to stay afloat if we adapt to meet the changing market. It's economics, boy!" Don explained. After a moment, he chuckled to himself, only then noticing his usage of the word "afloat."

Tanner tried to find the words to challenge his father, but was caught off guard as the *Kevin Costner* lurched to a halt. The sudden stop threw Tanner off his feet and he collapsed to the ground alongside the rocks and papers he had been referencing. Don felt his chest bruise as the wheel slammed into him. It was as if a giant hand had reached up out of the mire and grabbed hold of their vessel.

Reaching for the throttle, Don thought to increase the speed to brute force their way out of whatever mud-trap had gripped them. Tanner looked back to the line of ships they towed and saw the great dogwood one of their for affordable aquatic abodes had been pulling along. Its limbs, gnarled and torn, had twisted up into the boughs of some still-rooted tree.

"Dad, don't!" Tanner yelled.

But he was too late.

Don Hatfield had pushed the *Kevin Costner's* throttle as high as it would go.

Smoke plumed from what remained of *Kevin Costner*. Don Hatfield and his son Tanner sat, soaking wet, on the coastal flatland outside Crossville, Tennessee. For the first time in what seemed like years, Don was utterly silent. An assortment of ships now dotted the shore, torn and muddled up, rising from the murk like some kind of monument to what once was.

Decades of enterprise, trading, and renovating sat empty and ruined in front of the two men.

Tanner looked over as one of the waterlogged documents detailing their new financing plan floated up to meet them. He tried to pick it up, but the paper tore apart in his soft grip. Ink smeared across the section about the twenty-five percent interest rate. He closed his fist around it, wadding the small piece of what remained into a ball. He stood, tossing it into his father's lap before turning away to leave the scene. The dark water of the New Atlantic lapping against the shore the only sound between them until he finally spoke.

"Old world won't do us any good now, dad," he said.

Three Octobers
By Paige Hamm

About the author:

Having escaped the rising sea levels and flooded streets of Virginia Beach, VA, Paige is a new resident of Nashville. She has worked as an advocacy writer for multiple national and regional nonprofits and is a frequent haunt of the local library. Paige loves few things more than coffee, walks with her partner and their dogs Luna & Tidus, and rooting for all the sports teams of her new hometown.

Three Octobers
By Paige Hamm

One October -

The sky is gray over the site of their ceremony, but everyone assures her that rain means good luck on a wedding day. And what choice does she have but to believe them? She is a bride; she is impenetrable. A hurricane wouldn't dare to touch her three thousand dollar dress, nor overturn the strategically placed cocktail rounds. Surely storms would make concessions in the name of love, right?

A day on the road and hours later, the newlyweds eat sushi from a boardwalk restaurant. The sunset over the ocean looks puckered, as though an unseen force was leeching its energy. Further down the beach, palm trees are being covered with plastic wrap to protect them from high winds. They saunter back into the hotel, cocooned in newlywed bliss. The concierge waves them over and they say to themselves, how lovely—probably a bottle of celebratory champagne. Instead, he pushes a piece of hotel stationery across the counter. "It's evacuation orders," he says somberly. "You have two hours before they close the highways."

"But it's our honeymoon," she murmurs, as though the hurricane would cease its torrents for one bride.

Another October -

"Should we start packing?" she wonders aloud, picking at her cuticle.

"No, no," he reassures, with his eyes glued to the TV screen. "Not until it's looking like a Category 4." But then Jim Cantore arrives on the boardwalk, and she knows and the city knows it's time to go.

Later in the car, with suitcases covering the seats and their dog's ears perked up listening to the rising winds, she slams her feet into the brake pedal. "The library!" She gasps. "My books will be overdue!" Leapfrogging over sandbags, she hurdles to the returns' slot. She hadn't gotten to finish one of the books, but who knows how long the evacuation orders will last? It wasn't worth the late fee.

Another October, years later -

She watches the rain now, from behind windows in the foothills of Tennessee. Her fingers tighten around a coffee mug; will it happen again? Will the waters rise around her car and carry away the trash bin, the flower pots, the welcome mat as they did in Virginia?

But no—this time, the water flows down the hill and vanishes somewhere past her line of sight. She tells people how bad the flooding got back home, but people here just scratch their chins in disbelief. "Well, you're safe here in Tennessee," they tell her.

And she realizes how dangerous ignorance can be.

The Old Woman's Rocker: A Tall Tale

By Carter Allen

About the author:

Carter Allen lives in Nashville, Tennessee, with their wife, a jealous and vengeful housecat, and a rotating cast of strays.

The Old Woman's Rocker: A Tall Tale
By Carter Allen

The sky was gray as greed and hanging as low as a sow's belly when the neighbor came to her porch. The house was cleaned from stern to bow, the King crooned from the record player, and the old woman had just settled on her favorite recliner with a tall glass of–

"Sweet tea?"

"Oh, hell, no," the old woman snapped. "You think I'm a church lady? I used to drink it, sure, but the doctor told me to lay off on account of my blood sugar. I tried that Splenda stuff, but if you've tasted anything worse than *that* in a pitcher, I pity you. So I switched to rum and coke. Soothes my nerves." She did not, her neighbor had to admit, look like a particularly nervy person.

"We're getting ready to leave," the neighbor said, clearing his throat. "The weatherman said the river is like to rise, so we're headed for higher ground. There's a seat for you and your coke in the car if you'll come with us."

"A seat in the back, I reckon."

"You can sit up front. You can *drive*, long as you come.

This storm is nothing to tangle with. It's blown in from the Gulf, and it's liable to raise the river until we're all swimming. I'd hate for you to be here alone when the water comes."

"If the water comes to my door, I'll offer it a drink," she said, "and send it on its way."

"This isn't your usual rainmaker, Ma'am. This is a monster of a storm—"

"Now, listen here, and listen well, because I don't like to repeat myself. I've lived in this house my whole life. I raised my children in this house. My husband died right here in his favorite armchair. Tornadoes have tried to blow me away, heat waves have tried to melt me, men with money have tried to sweet-talk the ground out from under my feet, but through it all I've stayed. In all these years, that river has never thrown its banks. I'm going to sit right here, come what may, and I won't be moved."

With that, the old woman crossed her ankles like a debutante and raised her drink to toast.

Seeing that she couldn't be reasoned or reckoned with, the neighbor tipped his hat. The porch stairs creaking under his feet was the only goodbye he got.

"'You can ride up front.' Pah!" She took a fortifying gulp of her rum and coke. "Probably would've ended up babysitting those squirrely kids of his." Smacking her lips, she eased back in her threadbare recliner and began to rock. The rocker warbled with every lurch, sounding sorrier than a tone-deaf songbird on its last legs. To her tired ears, it was half a lullaby. Soon her eyelids drooped, her mouth rounded in a cavernous yawn, and she dozed off to the creaking of the rocker and the drizzle of rain.

She awoke to wet slippers.

At first, she thought herself dreaming. But as she blinked awake, she saw that her neighborhood had been transformed: the roads to canals, the mailboxes to buoys. Dark water lapped the base of her recliner, rain rattled overhead, and the wind screamed like a train whistle as it tore at the roof.

"Wait until those real estate men see this," she muttered, trying to settle the dread churning her belly into a whirlpool. "A waterfront property." She had half a mind to go inside and dry off, but she had told her neighbor that she wouldn't move. He wouldn't find her cowering in the attic come morning. She took a steeling sip of her rum and coke and tucked her feet beneath her.

That clapboard house was just as stubborn as its owner. As the water heaved, the house clung to its foundation. It might have won, too. But just then came a terrible *boom*—the sky ripping open, or a dam giving way, or some angry god breaking his promise never to drown the world again. She heard a low, distant roar, some unleashed beast growing closer and closer. With that, the water truly arrived.

The house groaned as it slipped its foundation. The wooden porch her husband had built with his own two hands splintered and shrieked. *Here it comes*, she thought, wrenching her eyes shut as her recliner slid toward the seething water. But that rocker had a lifetime guarantee to uphold. It smashed through the wooden railing, leaving upholstery scraps on the splinters. The house slid one way into the ravening river, and the recliner went the other, borne aloft on the waves.

Right about then floated by a bobcat, washed in from upriver and clinging to a sinking log. That cat was soaked through and looked ready to lie down and become a handsome spotted rug, but it pricked its tufted ears when it saw a fellow creature on a barge much more comfortable than its own. Gathering the last of its strength, it began cat-paddling towards the rocker.

"Oh, no you don't," the old woman moaned. She rifled through the recliner's pockets for a weapon but found only a few wadded tissues. She plunged her hand into the churning water and seized the recliner's lever, aiming to pop out the footrest and ward off the invader. But the footrest, a bit slow after forty years of service, didn't *pop* so much as *ease*. The bobcat saw only a welcome ramp. Grateful, it sunk its mighty claws into the footrest and dragged itself aboard.

This was too much. The old woman screamed and scuttled up the back of the recliner, which dipped perilously low under her weight, and raised the footrest. The bobcat, still shaky-legged from its swim, slid down into the seat, sending the old woman scurrying back up the footrest. When this threatened to capsize them, the cat scrambled to the headrest, lifting the old woman up and sending her tumbling back down the rocker.

The two of them chased each other 'round and the rocker see-sawed back and forth, threatening to dump them into the drink. This carried on until they both were half-seasick and mad with terror. Finally, the old woman collapsed in the recliner's seat, too wrung-out to move. The bobcat, just as weary, flopped down in her lap. It soaked her housedress through with river water, but that was a problem for tomorrow, should tomorrow come.

Together they sailed through the darkness.

Through that long and terrible night they saw a great many things: The water devouring the town it once had fed. The hands of the drowned reaching for heaven, the bodies of the dead turning in the waves. The old world heaving as it gave birth to the new. When it was too much to bear, the old woman closed her eyes and stroked the sodden fur of the trembling creature in her lap. On and on went the unmaking.

At long last—when the rain had died off to a trickle, then a mist, then nothing at all; when the water had had its way, and there was nothing left untouched; when the old woman had sensed her death a thousand times, only for Death to feint —the rocker struck solid ground.

One eye squinted open. Then the other. Ahead rose a grassy hump crowned with trees, some of which had even kept their leaves through the storm. This was, she realized, the very top of one of the rolling hills that ringed the town.

Her shipmate moved first. The bobcat disembarked down the footrest and sniffed at a clump of ferns. With a shake of its shovel-sized feet and a wag of its stump-tail goodbye, it threaded its way into the wood.

The old woman reached deep for a last kernel of strength to follow. She planted her slippered feet in the mud. Gnarled hands braced against the recliner's arms. She tried to stand, but her shaking legs couldn't carry her. Instead she sank to her knees and crawled up the slope, humble as a child. When she reached the top, she sat and gazed across the face of the water. Dawn lightened the heavy clouds, and here and there in the distance she could make out a jutting roof or a tangle of branches, but for every ruin that she recognized there were a hundred rendered strange and unknowable.

In time, others came to sit beside her. They were young and old, though none quite so old as she. They had clung to mattresses and rooftops and each other. They had all witnessed the end of the world, and they would carry this wound to the end of their days.

When the water receded, they would gather and talk: to recite the names of the dead and speak the miracles that had spared them. To share what knowledge they carried, and what ideas they had to shape the new world that was to be, for there could never be a return to what had been before the water came. But those words would come later. For now, they sat and watched in wonder as the morning light fell on the lake that had been home, too tired to weep or to sing.

Plankton and Bees

By J.J. Tyler

About the author:

J.J. Tyler is an emerging writer who loves his life as a dad and game developer in Gallatin, TN. He's become engrossed in writing as a creative outlet because if he doesn't get these ideas out of his head, he's afraid they'll build up a sizeable army and revolt. (It might be too late! Please send help!) When not working or writing, he overlooks his apartment complex, wearing blankets for capes and listening to "Something In The Way" with his daughter on their watch for evildoers.

Plankton and Bees
By J.J. Tyler

Buzz Bu—

First, it was the flowers. Nobody cared.

The grass withered.

The livestock perished.

The food supply dwindled.

We feigned concern while doing nothing. We ignored when the plankton all vanished from the sea. We ignored when the bees all stopped buzzing in the trees. We didn't question until our sea grew muted; the meadows became bare. After that, our ecosystem broke into a perpetual spiral we couldn't ignore—or repair.

We scraped by, fighting for nuts and seeds. Endless fighting for survival that escalated, where we hung bodies from trees—a grim monument to the plankton and bees.

The Collective
By Bobby Taylor

About the author:

Bobby Taylor traces his artistic roots back to grade school and a couple of special East Tennessee teachers. The cultural influences of the Mountain South, refracted by moonshine madness and Holy Ghost fire, fueled his need to express himself, which he has done in chart topping and Grammy-nominated songs, piles of poetry, and in dozens of theatrical productions including shows at the Lamb's Theater in New York City and the Ryman Auditorium. Bobby holds an MFA in Creative Writing from Naropa University's Jack Kerouac School of Disembodied Poetics. His writing has appeared in poetry collections *Not Enough Night*, *Sixfold*, *Semicolon 3.1*, and *Erasure*.

The Collective
By Bobby Taylor

A blue mist rises from the Nature Sphere Pond. Twenty-one-year-old Danny arrives in a golf cart with a vapor meter in his hand and a wrench in his back pocket. He waves his meter through the mist a few times till it beeps. He goes to the northern point of the pond, takes out his wrench, and turns a bolt until the mist dissipates and the frogs sound in a chorus of croaks, chirps, and trills like he grew up hearing on his grandfather's farm. He's reminiscing about catching catfish with the man who taught him about The Collective when he gets a call from his supervisor: "You need to go adjust the oxygen in the Aviary. Someone has managed to twist one of the valves. Birds are falling to the ground... couple of patrons fainted in there and have been carried outside it to get air. Hurry!"

"Sure," Danny says. "On the way."

Jennie Hooper, the Sphere's superintendent's daughter, is lying down with her head in her mother's lap when Danny gets to the Aviary. Before Jennie can open an eyelid and wink, Danny knows she's faking. He knows it was her who snitched a key, unlocked the valves, and changed the settings. It isn't the first time she's done this kind of thing.

Looking down at Jenny's mother, Danny asks, "Is she okay?"

"I think you know," says Mrs. Hooper, giving Danny a wave that sends him into the gym-sized aviary. He quickly adjusts the nitrogen and oxygen levels back to their normal ratio. He locks the valves, puts the Do Not Touch sign back in place, and steps out to Jennie and Mrs. Hooper.

"Can you sit with her a few minutes while I go find her some water?" asks Jennie's mother. Danny sits down, cradles Jennie's head in his lap, and strokes her hair.

The man-made creek breaks on the rocks close by; it joins the lush tall plants in sending rich oxygen into the air. Patrons continue milling about in the twenty-five-acre sphere. They take in the clean atmosphere that once was available for free in Boulder but now costs fifty credits for three hours inside the facility. Of course, if you work there, or have a green pass, you can spend whole days—breathing, walking, eating lunch at the cafe.

"I had to talk to you," Jennie whispers. "Daddy is being transferred. We're leaving tonight for the facility in Wyoming. You're coming."

"You know I can't... Your father—"

"You can stow away in the back of the shuttle," says Jennie. "When we get there, we'll run away. We can work with the underground to find a new place to start our life together." She shifts up on one elbow. "I know what you're going to say... that there's no reason to panic. But, Danny, the Asian Union is pulling out. The natural resources needed to keep the sphere alive are depleted and there's too much maintenance. Locals can't afford the admission. Most believers have given up on The Collective." She grasps his arm. "They're taking the carbon extractors—without them, nothing will survive. I'm not going without you!"

"All I know is Boulder," says Danny. "These mountains, the Flat Irons, the snow that used to fall, the trails I walked with my father. I can't go outside now without a mask, but this is home... Where I feel closest to The Collective."

"Ours will be the last shuttle to go. As Superintendent, Daddy can't leave until the investors and all the green badges have made it out." She squeezes his arm. "There will be no shuttles going or coming after that."

Danny gets out of an electric van and waves to the driver dropping him off at his apartment. He walks past his old 2025 Silverado that's been rotting in his driveway, like other dead gas-powered vehicles, for the last five years. He enters his apartment, takes off his mask, and sits down in front of his altar which consists of shards of crystal, his grandfather's New

Testament, a meditating buddha, a black candle, two red dice, a hawk feather, and the wedding rings of his mother and father—who joined The Collective when they perished in the heatwave.

He lights the candle, closes his eyes, and asks for guidance, for protection, for the strength to do what Jennie Hooper is asking him to do. A roll of the dice gives him double sixes—a message that his intuition is right—that he should stay in Boulder.

Back in her room at her father's house, Jennie is packing a backpack with the mood ring Danny gave her, her gold charm bracelet, a few clothes, and her journal that has become a prayer book. Her phone rings. "I'm sorry, I can't come," says Danny. "The spirits are telling me to stay here. I love you."

"You have to come, or else I'm staying here. If you're not coming, I'm coming to your apartment—"

The circuit fails. "Danny... Danny... Are you there?" She bows her head: "Ancestors, spirits, guides, life energy—hear my prayer—provide me with guidance, stealth, and strength." A wave of peace washes over her. She whispers, "Thank you! In the name of Gaia and all things good."

To prove she's boarded the shuttle, Jennie follows her mother to the bank of seats in the midsection. Her father is in the pilot's cabin preparing to speak as Jennie heads to the bathroom. The trapdoor is located just where she saw it was earlier when she hacked her daddy's info center and found out about it. She uses the key she stole from his masters to unlock the trap and then wiggles out onto the ground. Walking away, she knows that without a mask she will only have a half hour to make it to Danny's before she's overcome by the carbon in the air. She looks back at the shuttle as it's pulling away.

There, in a back window—face twisted in despair, tears flowing—is a regret-ridden Danny thinking *if only I had listened to The Collective*.

Tiny But Mighty
By Dana Fraedrich

About the author:

Dana Fraedrich is a dog lover, self-professed geek, and author of the steampunk fantasy series *Broken Gears*. Dana's books are full of secrets and colorful characters that examine the many shades of grey that paint the world. When she isn't busy writing or attending book festivals and conventions, she can be found playing video games, co-hosting the *Steam-Powered Movies* podcast, and educating fellow writers. Born and raised in Virginia, she earned her BFA from Roanoke College and is now carving out her own happily ever after in Nashville, TN with her husband. Dana is always writing; more books are on the way!

Tiny But Mighty
By Dana Fraedrich

Small, slender antennae and antennules swish through the muddy water of Mill Creek in Nashville, Tennessee. They send messages back to the automaton's silicon brain as it searches for its natural-born brothers and sisters. The tiniest of gears and other minuscule clockwork pieces click and spin and move as this mechanical *faxonius shoupi*—the Nashville Crayfish—goes about its mission. Sensors over the metal and transparent plastic carapace take readings of the water quality and other environmental factors, which automatically transmit back to the researchers who brought it here. Crayfish are an indicator species, serving as a warning system for when things go wrong within an ecosystem. This little mechanical version —designed toward the larger end of its representative species, which can get up to seven inches—exists to add the word "early" to that warning system.

On its journey, a passing bass comes to hover over the mechanical crayfish, which rears up, long claws open and ready to snap. The bass strikes, mouth open wide to engulf its prey. The pincers nip the bass right in the mouth, and the crayfish's tail fan shoots it backward in a flash, narrowly escaping becoming the bass's lunch. If the mechanical crayfish was eaten, though—and it wouldn't be the first time—its researcher-handlers would follow the tracker inside its body to retrieve it, all while the crayfish took the opportunity to gather some helpful readings from inside the bass.

The mechanical crayfish eventually homes in on a group of its chitinous brethren clustered beneath a large slab of limestone. They are social little creatures, and a handful of another species—some Saddle Crayfish—have joined them in their murky little hideaway. Cogwheels and springs twitch and whir, expand and contract, as the mechanical crayfish scuttles against the current, over small rocks and past a curious dace or two, to reach its targets.

"How do you do, fellow crayfish," it seems to say. Or at least that's how one of the researchers has described this interaction. Crayfish groups develop linear hierarchies amongst themselves. Presenting subordinate chemical signals and behaviors helps avoid fights with its more dominant, snappier brethren. But should another crayfish square up to the synthetic version, gears inside its metal-jointed legs would reverse and it would walk backward in a show of surrender.

The mechanical crayfish takes readings from and video of its natural-born fellows. It can also attach tiny trackers to them, all of which will help the researchers to monitor the health of the crayfish as well as the overall health of Mill Creek. With creations like this assisting in monitoring and conservation efforts, real-time data can catch issues as they begin, which can also help lead to the source of those issues, whether it be dumping, run-off from elsewhere, or other causes.

These clockwork versions of animals have been deployed the world over and are useful in solving a multitude of problems. Tiny mechanical wasps monitor re-wilding efforts in the Amazon Rainforest, mainly around where fig trees have been planted. Mechanized Tasmanian devils in Tasmania and New South Wales distribute treatments for DFTD. Cheetahs made of fur and metal are used for semen collection and later insemination to increase genetic variability in the species.

Our mechanical crayfish once even met a spring-loaded alligator snapping turtle. These iconic reptiles, once victims of the exotic pet trade and, like so many other species, habitat destruction, have come back thanks to the myriad pieces of protection legislation passed only through the tireless dedication and relentless effort of far too few.

The struggle continues. There are those wishing to cut the funding given to research and conservationist organizations that develop and deploy these clockwork assistants. There are also those who wish to roll back those regulations instated to prohibit the use of these magnificent mechanical marvels in military applications.

It has taken time, setbacks, hard work, persistence, and cooperation, but our world is on the upswing. Mill Creek is a microcosm of what is possible all over our planet. As the mechanical crayfish makes its rounds up and down this single waterway, it serves as an ambassador between humankind and crustacean kin. Through its engineered eyes and other synthetic senses, we see the world from a crayfish's perspective. We can observe in real time its quality of life, which informs how our own will be directly affected. The Nashville Crayfish, this unique, tiny but mighty species, has become a symbol of resilience, fortitude, and hope.

The author would like to thank the Nashville Zoo and the folks behind the Nashville Crayfish Project for their assistance in researching for this story and for all the amazing work they're doing to preserve this incredible, little critter.

Treasure Hunting at the End of the World
By Brenna Marie

About the author:

While Brenna Marie spends her days pouring through institutional data and corralling three dogs, she most enjoys the time she and her husband spend watching their infant daughter learn to walk, talk, and so much more. This is her first short story publication.

Treasure Hunting at the End of the World
By Brenna Marie

Dust motes float around Cameron's head as he expertly navigates us through the winding, narrow chasm. These giant fissures only started forming throughout the Spanish countryside in the past decade, and mapping the labyrinthine cracks was impossible thanks to continuing shifts in the arid landscape. We're diving headfirst into a foolish endeavor. He knows it, and I know it. But the call of treasure is tantalizing. What treasure would be worth enduring scorching heat, relentless sandstorms, and crippling dehydration? The ridicule of our colleagues and probably the respect of our friends? Nothing less than the great treasure of Hernán Cortés.

Not a city of shimmering gold or a pitiful trove of conquistador riches, though. After all, the world no longer needs precious metals, gems, or works of art. We're fighting for survival in an increasingly hostile environment. One hellbent on showing humanity the terrible price for its hubris and greed. Experts on such things say we can probably hold out another fifty years if the current agricultural hubs maintain suitable water and heat levels. Even longer if scientists can create heartier and less water-dependent versions of edible crops. In fact, my brother is currently running the Department of Scientifically Altering Potatoes, or something along those lines. I'm proud of him. Any breakthroughs his department makes could increase the likelihood of human survival on this dangerously hot and unsympathetic planet.

I like to think I am on an equally important mission. Because we shouldn't settle for mere survival on heartier, bland potatoes. No. The world needs us to succeed on this harrowing journey. We need something to live *for*.

Cameron signals a halt and pulls up his UV protective goggles to better read the rock striations. Despite the cracks being recent, the cave system we're searching for formed millennia ago, but with all the momentous environmental upheavals in the last hundred years it may have shifted lower in the Earth's crust. Looking for the usual geological traits would only help us so far.

To be honest, we aren't sure what we will find, if anything. The texts describing the location of Cortés's treasure are more... *mythic* in nature than the hard, scientific facts our colleagues prefer. But I can feel in my bones that we are close. After years of searching, we are on the cusp of discovery.

"I can see a natural well ahead," Cameron says after surveying the landscape. "Hopefully it's deep enough."

"Let's press on before another dust-storm picks up," I reply eagerly. Cameron may have the geology/botany/meteorology skills that got us this far, but I bring superior spelunking skills to the table.

After securing the anchor and preparing my gear, I descend into the mouth of a well only three feet wide. Natural wells like this are our best chance at finding the cave we are looking for. To our best knowledge, the treasure cavern would have several wells connected to it, acting as natural air shafts. Cave-ins would have likely shut off most, if not all, of these access points, but the closer we can get without having to waste time and energy digging would help immensely.

I make it about fifty feet down with no change in the width of the well. By this point there should have been some change in size, whether larger or smaller. The uniformity of the well is both unnerving and thrilling. This is no natural formation. At least, not anymore. Someone took an already established well and *carved out* the walls to maintain a steady width for at least fifty feet! I examine the walls and see no signs of blasthole or gear marks. Any indication of the type of engineering used to create this shaft has long since eroded away. My heart starts racing. *This is it.*

The shaft abruptly ends only a few feet further down. Once I establish the stability of the rock layer, I pull on the rope, letting Cameron know it is safe to descend. I'm too excited to wait for him to make it all the way down before rattling off my speculations and hopes at top speed.

"Calm down, Kit," Cameron grunts as he hugs the wall, sliding down a foot at a time. "It's hard for me to focus on not dying with you jabbering at me like a monkey." Sadly, the phrase would be lost on many younger generations today.

They're just another in an ever-expanding list of extinct species now, but I am old enough to at least have *heard* of a monkey.

"How can I be calm? This must be it! There is no other reason for a well this perfectly symmetrical and uniform to be here. This area was too rocky for farmland. There weren't minerals that mining operations would deem worth the effort. It had to have been them!"

"Ah yes, monks are known for their great feats of engineering," Cameron jokes, still about twenty feet above me.

"Alright, it may not have been the monks themselves, but they could have paid someone to do this. They needed these wells structurally sound to maintain the cavern and protect their secret!" I jump up and down lightly, careful not to disrupt the rock formations below.

My jumping causes my flashlight helmet to dip down, light flashing off a small, weirdly shaped rock near the wall. As Cameron struggles to make it down the last dozen feet, I pick up the rock to get a better look. After a little dusting it is clear that this isn't a rock at all, it's the desiccated shell of a bean.

In a panic, I grab the pickaxe from my belt and start digging into the rock.

Cameron is yelling at me to stop, but I can't make out the words over my internal denial. *It can't be gone! Not after we got so close!* I put all my hope, despair, frustration, and fear into a flurry of swings. I throw out all guidelines of how to excavate without destroying the structural integrity. I just have to get through. I have to find it.

My swings crescendo with a *POP,* and a burst of stale air blasts from the opening. But that's not all.

The sweet, bitter smell hits me like a wave and I know before opening my eyes. It is here. Brought overseas by ships from the New World, reforged, and meticulously preserved these thousands of years by the ancient order of monks. The beans are gone, but this may be even better.

We've found it. Stacked at least fifty feet high in ingots the length of my forearm, the treasure of Hernán Cortés. Chocolate!

The Vines

By C. L. Nicholson

About the author:

C. L. Nicholson is a native Nashvillian who works as a freelance book editor and magazine writer. A longtime fan of science fiction and fantasy, she occasionally puts down her current book obsession to wrangle weeds in her backyard garden. She can be contacted through her website, CLNicholson.com.

The Vines
By C. L. Nicholson

Ruth sat back in a heap, wiping the sweat that dripped in sheets off her face. She had spent two hours battling the hissing vines invading the back garden, digging them up at the roots and then dropping the greyish-green plants into the vinegar bucket. A vinegar bath was the only way to kill the vines, apparently—pure, straight vinegar. If you dropped a vine on the ground, it would re-root within minutes, its suckers digging into the soil with the quiet hissing the plant made when it moved.

Looking around the vineless garden, she wasn't completely satisfied. It was hard to be satisfied with the weak, scrubby vegetables left in the beds, but she did have the assurance of a job well done. Or at least good enough done. Her phone had been blaring heat advisory warnings all morning, but she had pressed through the scorching temperatures long enough to make sure her peppers would live to see another day.

Peppers were just about all that would grow in these hot summers. She had hoped for a few tomatoes, carefully tending this year's Romas and beefsteaks, faithfully measuring out the water from her rain barrel for them each day. And then the city had gotten eight inches of rain in twenty-four hours. Soon the tomatoes showed the telltale bruising of end rot; she had lost all of them so far, and the few blossoms left were withering in the August heat.

So she tended her jalapeños, although any gratitude she had felt for them had long been replaced by bitterness. She had canned them and frozen them. She made pepper jelly and pepper bread and pickled peppers. She wanted to leave the rest of the peppers to rot on the vine, but with produce scarce in the stores, she needed to harvest what she could.

Ruth lifted her hat and wiped away more sweat from her forehead. She was fighting a losing battle there; she was already drenched under her arms and her breasts, sweat trickling down from everywhere to who-knows-where.

At least the hissing vine battle was at a truce for the day.

Pushing herself up off the ground, Ruth looked at the heavy bucket of vinegar. She was tempted to leave it where it sat. Her back ached from bending over the garden beds all morning. She started to walk away, but then she pictured some animal tipping the vinegar and spilling the vine, undoing all her work. She went back and picked up the bucket.

Hissing vines had to soak in vinegar for three days before they would die. Everyone hoped that solution would keep working. When the vine had first been noticed spreading quickly across farms, *they*—the government, corporations, whoever—had tried industrial sprays, which killed almost everything except the vine. They tried spraying vinegar, too, but soaking was the key.

People said it would get better now that they knew what to do. Ruth hoped it would. Food was getting expensive since so many fields had been lost. There was talk of FEMA distributing MREs.

As Ruth hauled her vinegar bath toward the shed, she pondered what an MRE would taste like and whether peppers would improve the taste. She chuckled at the thought and then tripped, stumbling over a root she hadn't seen. The vines hissed at the agitation, and vinegar sloshed out over the bucket.

"No!" she shouted in a strangled voice. She put the bucket on the ground and got down to search for any escaped plants. She shook her head at her carelessness as she crawled, spilled vinegar soaking into her jeans.

Ruth raked her hands carefully through the grass. All the vines still seemed to be in the bucket, their hissing now barely audible as they calmed. She got up slowly, carefully rising onto her knees before standing; she was lightheaded after all that excitement. She picked up the bucket again, and this time she made it all the way to the shed, where she fastened a lid over the vinegar bath and tucked it away in a corner.

She shut the shed door and leaned against it, closing her eyes in relief. She was thirsty; she could feel the day getting hotter. It was probably lunchtime by now, but the thought of food turned her stomach.

Probably all those peppers in the omelet this morning, she decided.

She opened her eyes and tried to stand up straight, but a

wave of dizziness made her stumble back against the shed. She breathed deeply, hoping it would pass, trying to calm her racing heart. She focused on the sound of her breath, the inhales and exhales hissing slowly.

Hissing.

Ruth held her breath. The hissing continued. She glanced at the garden and saw a tendril of a vine reaching into a bed as if to caress the pepper plant in front of it.

"No!" she cried again, running toward the vine, jerking it up and away from her peppers.

She pulled frantically, following the vine farther from the garden. She wrapped the loose end around her arm to keep it from trailing on the ground as she searched for the roots. Spying where the plant disappeared into the dirt, she pushed the coiled vine further up her shoulder and kneeled to pierce the soil with her spade.

Her head throbbed and her hands shook as she lifted small piles of dirt and tossed them aside. *At least I'm not sweating anymore*, she thought, relieved to not be wiping her face every five seconds.

Finally, she pulled the roots free, the vine hissing in anger as she lifted it from the dirt triumphantly with her parched, red hands. She smiled weakly and looked up into the blazing sunlight, half expecting applause. She felt the vine's coils shift around her body, and her vision grew blurry. As she tumbled to the ground, her landing was much softer than she expected. The vines were quiet as they welcomed her.

The Tree
By Joe Sedita

About the author:

Joe Sedita is a retired CPA. He lives near Sewanee, Tennessee with his wife, Paula, and four-footed friends, Gabby, Peach, and Stella. He is enrolled in the MTSU Write mentorship program.

The Tree
By Joe Sedita

One hundred cold seasons ago, I fell as a seed from my mother's embrace to the perfect spot for my nursery, moist fertile soil. The opening in the canopy above allowed me to receive abundant warmth and light from father sun. My roots grew deep. I was nourished by the tumbled trunks of my ancestors. My thirst was quenched by spray from the stream that tumbled down the hillside beside me. I was comforted by the touch of my family, rooted in the ground around me. The wind rocked me and taught me to dance. Birds made their homes in my branches, raised their young, and spread my seeds to distant places. Green mosses dressed me. I was home to life as the forest was home to me.

One day, a man came. He brought flame and heat and pain. My green cloak turned to ashes. The birds abandoned me. The wind blew but there was no more dancing.

My family is all gone. Only the topmost of my leaves remain. Ruined. I console myself knowing that I will soon be home to life again—worms and bugs and things that burrow underground. My body will disappear like winter snow that melts into the ground with the spring thaw. Mankind will never know—or care—that I lived.

Wolves have dominion over what once was paradise. Now it lies destroyed—betrayed, displaced by calloused hearts and blind, deceiving eyes. What can tomorrow hold? My only hope is that my seed, released by fire and heat, may rise again —home to life, in spite of them.

Doom Loop

By Chase Stowell

About the author:

Nashville Born, Bred, and Resident, Chase Stowell is the editor at *Impossible Worlds*, a quarterly sci-fi/fantasy magazine.

Doom Loop
By Chase Stowell

You awaken in your sleep pod, bustle outside your alcove rising with the sun as the day begins. Science refers to your era as the Ordovician but you're ignorant of a term you will never know from hundreds of millions of years in the future. You feel the cool water surrounding your body as you leave your alcove and swim down the corridor. Your mind pushes away the thought that every day has been colder than the last. A fresh chill runs up your spine as you round a corner at the sight you encounter. A sloping corridor to a higher level that you take all the time is dry. Bone dry. Impassable. You desperately don't want to think about how much of the structure is sticking up above the water line now. Considering how close this is to your current home, how the algae everyone eats has long been dying off, how close the ice is at this point, reality was no longer permitting you ignorance. The bio-glass that makes up your cities, excreted by a trilobite that might leave a few fossils, is destined to dissolve in the seas when they return. How could any one of you have know these vast underwater cities are bouncing more and more sunlight back into space as more and more buildings went up. Death by sprawl. Your civilization is going to disappear with no evidence that you were ever here. You sit under the water's edge, feeling your body growing colder and colder. Maybe they'll get it right next time.

You awaken in your anemone, the din outside your coral rising with the sun as the day begins. Science refers to your era as the Devonian but how would you know? No one's doing that for three hundred million years. The rocks that will one day form the cap of the Cumberland Plateau had been laid down in the shallow sea that formed your home. It was harder to breathe when you woke up today. Again. You swim more slowly, same as everyone around, same as it had been for too many days now. Bordering on drifting, punctuated by weak movement to maintain momentum, though why anyone bothered became less and less clear. Yesterday, you learned that the last of the reef builders had died off. Cystoidea (you also found them easier to harvest, attached to the sea floor than their cousins the starfish) that made up most of your diet were likely not far behind. You search your memory for the last time that someone flashed you a toothless smile but you have to hug your soft, squishy body closer as the thought of joy was too distant to recall. Who could have foreseen overproducing both species would have negative side effects? Your culture will collapse ignorant that many, many species in the ocean require oxygen, the same as you. A vast sea of people who only considered what other animals could do for you, not how the vast web of life connects and how delicate that web is. And now? Your nation vanishes with nary a footprint. Life on land completely unaware of your passing. You drift languidly forward, drawn on by nothing, quietly gasping. Maybe they'll get it right next time.

You awaken in your sleeping quarters, buzz outside your hill fort rising with the sun as the day begins. Science refers to your era as the Permian but not for a quarter billion years. The entire area has been slowly lifted over two thousand feet above sea level and erosion has begun to shape the landscape into something that will be recognizable at some future point. You feel the heat wash on your face, though summer is not for some time. You can see dark smoke billowing in the distance as you emerge from the fort. The smell of rotten eggs hangs in the air as it has for many weeks after the sky lit up and a rumble was heard from impossibly far away to the south. The fishermen had long stopped going to the coast as there was no fish for them. You pull your hood up over your head as you feel the sun burning what skin is exposed. Was the sun always this hot? The elders insist that it wasn't but who knows if they're right? The sages had been saying that the sky is thinner, storms are worse and that harnessing the volcanoes for power was a mistake. No one listens to them.

Perhaps that was a mistake. You survey the horizon and confirm that the report is the same as yesterday. Nearly everything is dying. You could smile darkly that your people are not leaving this world alone. Irony aside, you can not describe this process as great. The plants you all manipulated to grow into your homes and the surrounding forests would be interred across these mountains. How could any of the individuals that made up your tiny family be picked out of a mass of future coal seams? You dip back into the shade of your home and stare hollowly in the distance, looking but not really taking anything in. Maybe they'll get it right next time.

You awaken in your hut, the exodus outside your village rising with the sun as the day begins is not relevant to the journey ahead of you. You feel the summer heat pound on your body as you leave your village. The collective hope is that you all reach the huge lake on the other side of the mountain range to the south. Your people don't call either the Gulf of Mexico nor the Appalachian Mountains. That's for the future. You all have chosen to abandon the one hundred million year old river that had once been a sea, as it no longer serves its function in this sweltering climate. The use of volcanic energy by your society was even more intense than it had been in previous eras. The raging lava flows in your backyard created areas to avoid on your journey and choked out the sky but the areas north and west had grown even more dry than your current home. As you pack, you pause to regard a small leathery creature that was observing you and your kin with curiosity. Many of its cousins had picked off your relatives but largely avoided your community. You could defend yourselves and planned to do so during your travels. But as your eyes meet that of the little beast you can almost make out what it would say if it had language you could comprehend. "The future is ours." Maybe. Your people would have to concede to these terrible lizards. Maybe they'll get it right next time.

You awaken in your bed, avian dinosaurs outside your home rising with the sun as the day begins. Science refers to your era as the Cretaceous but sixty-six million years passes before anyone thinks to call it that. You look up again and confirm that yes, the tiny star you spotted a few weeks ago continues to be visible in the daytime and is much larger than it had been. You will never be given the opportunity to comprehend everything that will happen when it strikes the Earth. Sure, you'll feel the ground shake beneath you in a way you've never felt before. You might have the barest amount of time to visually take in the column of debris reaching into space. You will likely be long dead, your home engulfed in flames. And if that doesn't get you, then the debris raining back down would certainly bury you and everyone you've ever known. If by some miracle neither of those results destroy you and your country, the hope of surviving the darkness of clouds now covering the planet was virtually non-existent for a creature of your size. Any plants that had been in your diet or any animals that rely on those plants that you may have eaten would've quickly died off, leaving you to starve. A forced winter is here and all is ashes. It would've never occurred to you that small rat-like creatures that plagued your food supplies would be the inheritors of the world that your death would vacate. This time is not your fault. Some events are truly outside our control. But a thin hope can still hang in the air. Maybe they'll get it right next time.

You awaken in your bedroom, traffic noise outside your apartment rising with the sun as the day begins. Science refers to your era as the Quaternary but you're not a geologist nor does your work require you to retain a term you heard in passing at school decades ago. You feel the summer heat wash on your face as you leave your apartment and get into your car. Your mind doesn't connect the feeling with action as the one causing the other. As you idle in the drive-thru, a line of cars on either end boxing you in, you hope that it's not ninety in October again this year. Your early start lets you park under one of the trees in the vast sea of asphalt surrounding the squat brick building you pass most of your week in. You swear you can hear the dull roar of I-65 even this far from the exit. After you finish your coffee, the autopilot that's been engaged for hours since you woke up switches off and you hesitate by the trash can. Your hand shifts six inches to the left and deposits the paper cup in the recycle bin. Maybe you could make a few different choices today.

Afterword

When I was in graduate school, my argumentation professor wanted us to complete the C-ROADS climate simulator. Each person in the class was assigned a country for whom they would represent as a climate delegate, and our goal was to negotiate amongst ourselves things such as our country's peak year of emissions, the year we begin reducing emissions, our annual reduction rate, and our efforts to prevent deforestation and promote afforestation in order to reduce the global temperature increase by 2100 from the projected 3.3°C to 1.5°C. Other students represented India, China, countries from the European Union, and a slew of countries from categories of "other developed nations" and "other developing nations." I, however, was assigned the United States of America, and I took this seminar in spring of 2020, when Donald Trump was president, months after US began the process of withdrawing from the Paris Climate Accords. So my role was a bit different than others. While they were offering trade and energy deals and explaining how their efforts were worth X, Y, and Z to other countries, I was an agent of chaos, set on extracting as many resources as I could while making promises for change that I, perhaps too optimistically, hoped my country would honor. At the end of the first day, progress had been made, cutting the initial 3.3°C increase to 2.1°C. By the end of the second day, however, nations in Africa, South America, and the Middle East, tired of being manipulated and exploited by the larger countries, withdrew from the arrangement altogether, telling the US, EU, China, and India that they would have to solve it themselves. Suffice to say, we did not, and my professor told us it was the first time he had ever had a group end up raising the projected the global temperature increase on the second day.

Roughly a year later, I had a short story published—my second ever. This was a short piece (one that an author in this anthology and the illustrator insisted I include, so look for that below) in which I asked what would aliens intent on colonizing other worlds think of a planet wrecked by climate change. This story was in part a response to my experience with the C-ROADS simulator, where it was clear that in order to make any large change, it would take a coordinated effort on a global scale to reduce the impacts. It felt hopeless, and as Em articulated so well in the foreword, I was mourning the loss of the future.

Then something shifted. It was not immediate. I didn't wake up one day and suddenly lose all worry over the world my daughter would grow up in—I doubt that worry will ever go away. But I wrote and engaged with more ecofiction. I consumed works by Paolo Bacigalupi, Bong Joon-ho, Octavia

E. Butler, Ray Bradbury, Kim Stanley Robinson, N.K. Jemisin. Their ecofiction was not always positive, but it was not always negative either. Rather, the speculative stories they told were an intervention. So often, our climate crisis is framed through partisan policy debates, dense jargon, and abstract numbers. Ecofiction brings it closer, makes it tangible. Speculative fiction allows the audience to ask, *"What if my world were like that?"* These authors not only depicted various ecological crises but also how people continued living. They made me feel the loss, the urgency, *and* the possibilities. I found that, through ecofiction narratives, I could imagine not only the collapse but also resilience, which is what I needed in the increasing precarious world in which we live.

That was the motivating idea for this anthology, and the stories by these incredible authors do just that. They range from hopeful to devastating, comedic to heart-wrenching, but they all offer insights into how life continues, in spite of it all. In ordering the stories, I chose to begin and end with stories that follow a trajectory of hopelessness to harboring even the faintest glimmer of hope. The stories between these draw out themes of the commercialization of survival, the mounting agricultural issues of our continually heating world, the extinction of what we have known and the embrace of what we don't, and the bonds we must forge to keep hope alive— to keep from burning out while there is still more to be done.

It is my sincere hope that someone picks up this anthology and begins their own journey of reflection on what ecofiction can do for us, personally, and for the world. Ecofiction will not solve the climate crisis, but it can help us process grief, spark imagination, and remind us that we are not alone in our struggle to make sense of an uncertain future. We will continue our mourning of what we will inevitably lose, but through these stories and others, ecofiction demonstrates that there are still choices to be made, lives to live, futures to fight for, and a radical hope of imagining what could be. Hope, particularly in trying times like these, may seem like naïve optimism. In reality, as made clear through these narratives and others, hope can be an insistence that our stories aren't over yet.

M.A. Dosser

March 10, 2025

Long-Term Scans
By M.A. Dosser

This story was originally published by 101 Words *in October 2021.*

"What do the readings show?"

"Short-term scans indicate compatibility. Ample land above sea level. Plentiful natural and bioengineered vegetation and livestock. An adaptable atmosphere."

"Perfect! We should inform Command."

"Long-term scans, however, indicate increased instances of extreme weather. Heat waves, droughts, fires across all continents. Dangerous precipitation events occurring multiple times a cycle. Polar vortexes weakening, pushing frigid air into temperate climes. The oceans have an average pH value of 7.6 —few marine organisms thrive. Low sentient population likely due to these issues."

"What is your assessment?"

"Nonviable for colonization."

"Damn. Well, cross Earth off the list. We'll keep looking."

Special thanks are due to more people than I have space for here. The biggest thanks goes to the Curb Center for Art, Enterprise, and Public Policy at Vanderbilt University, particularly Rachel Thompson, who helped shepherd this idea from its conception to completion, and David Wilson, who kept me on track with all the financials. If it were not for the Curb Center's generous Creative Inquiry Grants, this anthology would never have happened. Hopefully you enjoy the anthology as much as I do and volume two isn't too far away.

Thomas J. Griffin and Em Palughi volunteered their very valuable time to speak at the Writing Ecofiction for Tomorrow's World workshop I coordinated. Their presentations on ecogrief and thematic writing not only taught the participants a lot, but it shaped how I went about editing this anthology. It also helped produce stories that appear in these pages, as multiple authors were attendees. Their contributions open the anthology, and I couldn't have asked for a better start. While they set the bar high, the other authors deliver. To all the authors included here, thank you for trusting me with your stories.

This anthology's gorgeous cover and interior art sprang from the mind of the great Kevin Pabst. Kevin finished the last piece of art just two days before he and his wife welcome their his first son into the world. Even with that looming deadline, each piece is beautiful enough to hang in a museum.

Alex Robinson and Tom Eisenbraun, our times talking about potential music, sound design, and performances of an audio version of the anthology had me more excited and more engaged in creating new work than I have been in a long time. I don't drink coffee, but I would gladly grab a cup with you two any time.

Additional thanks are owed to my colleagues in Vanderbilt University's Department of Communication Studies and the editors of *Spitfire Magazine* at Vanderbilt for helping to spread the word about the anthology to students, faculty, staff, and other community members. I met and emailed a lot of great people from other departments and colleges in the greater Nashville area, so thank you all for helping to make this anthology as great as it could be, and I apologize for sending you so many emails.

Lastly, Brenna and Sophie. You two had to put up with me spending our weekends retreating to my office to read submissions, send emails, copyedit, send more emails, do layout, and all other things associated with this anthology, and you supported me through it all. Between everything else going on in our first year in Nashville, I often felt like things were too much, and you always made me feel better. Thank you for your unending support and love.

About the Editor:

M.A. Dosser is the co-founder and editor of *Flash Point SF* and a senior lecturer of communication studies at Vanderbilt University. On any given day he's either researching speculative fiction fandoms, teaching public speaking, or writing about heroic blueberries, raven knights, and long voyages in outer space. You can read more about his creative and scholarly work at maxdosser.com.

About the Foreword Author:

Em Palughi is a queer ecopoet from South Alabama. You can find her work in *Gulf Coast, Black Warrior Review, Foglifter, The Southern Poetry Anthology: Alabama, Apricity Press,* and elsewhere She was the winner of the 2025 Plentitudes Poetry Prize and a finalist in the 2023 Saints and Sinners Poetry Prize, the 2023 Tennessee Willians Literary Festival Poetry Prize, and the 2024 Lit/South Awards. She has an MFA in Poetry from Vanderbilt University where she was awarded the 2024 Kathryn Sedberry Prize.

About the Illustrator:

Kevin Pabst is artist, musician, and father to a newborn son and 19-year-old one-eyed dog. When he's not making concert posters, album covers, or children's book illustrations, he teaches communication classes at a local community college. You can see his work at www.kevinpabstdesign.com.

www.ingramcontent.com/pod-product-compliance
Lightning Source LLC
Chambersburg PA
CBHW060235180626
46813CB00007B/3093